MW01004236

The NOT So

Dial Books for Young Readers

Quiet LIBRARY

ZACHARIAH OHORA

Every Saturday, Oskar and Theodore got up bright and early.

Not to watch cartoons, or play
outside with their friends.
It was the day they went . . .

. . . to the library with Dad!

Dad always said that a day of quiet exploration required a proper breakfast.

At the library, Theodore and Oskar returned their
old books, waved to Ms. Watson, and crept past
old pickled-onion Mr. Tasker.

They headed down to the children's department while Dad headed up to the nap department.

Oskar and Theodore were just settling into another quiet library day when — BOOM! CRASH! GROWL!

It appeared there was a monster in the library.

They couldn't outrun the monster,

so they tried hiding,

They even tried trapping the monster,

but that just made him angrier.

The many-headed monster had tried everything to make books taste good.

Seymour topped his with whipped cream.

This book tastes terrible!

Chuck tried mustard.

YUCK!

WELL, WE'LL JUST HAVE TO EAT YOU GUYS INSTEAD!
GRAB THE SPRINKLES, WINSTON!

That's when Theodore
remembered something.

Luckily, monsters like story time
as much as they like donuts.

After story time, the monster promised to clean up the library. Besides, Ms. Watson could really use some help reaching the high shelves.

The boys promised to return for story time every Saturday.
(After Bob, Seymour, Winston, Pat, and Chuck promised
not to eat them!)

And that's how the not so quiet library
became quiet again.

For the Old Man and the Librarians of the Manchester Public Library
and a shout-out to Ferretti's Grocery Store Bakery Department

Dial Books for Young Readers
Penguin Young Readers Group
An imprint of Penguin Random House, LLC
375 Hudson Street
New York, NY 10014

Copyright © 2016 by Zachariah OHora

Penguin supports copyright. Copyright fuels creativity, encourages diverse voices,
promotes free speech, and creates a vibrant culture. Thank you for buying an authorized
edition of this book and for complying with copyright laws by not reproducing, scanning,
or distributing any part of it in any form without permission. You are supporting writers
and allowing Penguin to continue to publish books for every reader.

Library of Congress Cataloging-in-Publication Data
Names: OHora, Zachariah, author.
Title: The not so quiet library / by Zachariah OHora.
Description: New York, NY : Dial Books for Young Readers, [2016] | Summary:
"Oskar and and his bear Theodore must save the day when an angry monster barges into
the library...and thinks it's an all-you-can-eat buffet!"—Provided by publisher.
Identifiers: LCCN 2015026297 | ISBN 9780803741409 (hardback)
Subjects: | CYAC: Libraries—Fiction. | Books and reading—Fiction. |
Monsters—Fiction. | Bears—Fiction. | BISAC: JUVENILE FICTION / Books &
Libraries. | JUVENILE FICTION / Monsters. | JUVENILE FICTION / Humorous Stories.
Classification: LCC PZ7.O41405 Np 2016 | DDC [E]—dc23 LC record available at http://lccn.loc.gov/2015026297

Printed in China
3 5 7 9 10 8 6 4 2

Design by Lily Malcom • Text set in Egyptian Slate Pro

The artwork was created using acrylic paint
on Stonehenge printmaking paper.